Grandma's House

Written by Kirsten Hall

Illustrated by Gloria Calderas

My First READER

children's press®

A Division of Scholastic Inc.
New York Toronto London Auckland Sydney
Mexico City New Delhi Hong Kong
Danbury, Connecticut

Library of Congress Cataloging-in-Publication Data

Hall, Kirsten.
  Grandma's house / written by Kirsten Hall ; illustrated by Gloria Calderas.
      p. cm. — (My first reader)
Summary: A young girl enjoys visiting her grandmother so much that she wishes she could stay.
  ISBN 0-516-24411-6 (lib. bdg.)   0-516-25502-9 (pbk.)
  [1. Grandmothers–Fiction. 2. Stories in rhyme.] I. Calderas Lim, Gloria, ill. II. Title. III. Series.
  PZ8.3.H146Gr 2004
  [E]–dc22
                                    2003014073

Text © 2004 Nancy Hall, Inc.
Illustrations © 2004 Gloria Calderas.
All rights reserved.
Published in 2004 by Children's Press, an imprint of Scholastic Library Publishing.
Published simultaneously in Canada.
Printed in China.

15 16 17 18 19 R 22 21 20 19 18   62
Scholastic Inc., 557 Broadway, New York, NY 10012.

Note to Parents and Teachers

Once a reader can recognize and identify the 27 words used to tell this story, he or she will be able to successfully read the entire book. These 27 words are repeated throughout the story, so that young readers will be able to recognize the words easily and understand their meaning.

The 27 words used in this book are:

and	house	talk
both	I	that
cheek	kiss	to
could	love	today
dog	loves	walk
go	nap	we
grandma's	play	will
her	soft	wish
hide-and-seek	stay	with

4

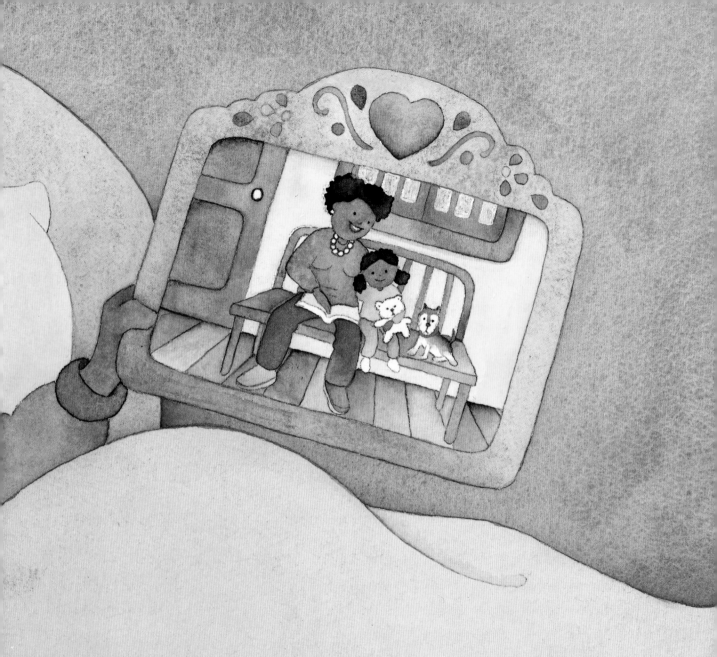

I love grandma's house.

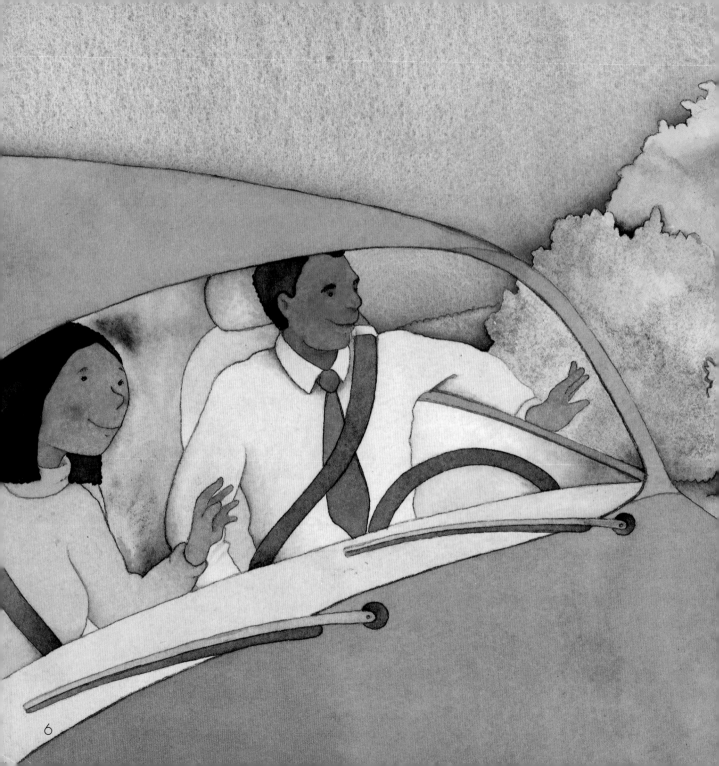

6

I will go today.

We play with her dog.

Her dog loves to play.

I love grandma's house.

We both love to walk.

We will walk her dog.

We will walk and talk.

I love grandma's house.

We play hide-and-seek.

We both love to nap.

I kiss her soft cheek.

We both love to play.

I wish that I could stay.